My Grandpa the Eidi Man

by Zara Suliman

It is the night before Eid.

Our house is full of busy
bees, hustling and bustling
to get everything ready
for Eid.

My mum has bundled herself
with never ending holiday
checklists.

My dad is buzzing around
on his phone, as he invites
friends and families.

My sister is fussing with her
clothes and jiggling with all her
jewelleries.

...And as for me?

welllll!

I am doing what I do every year, the night before Eid.
That is waiting for my grandpa to turn up...

Although, I never get to catch him.
Somehow, I get tired of waiting for him and doze off.

...And usually, I see him on the morning of Eid.

Sometimes, I wonder why that is so...

Each year, my mum gives different reasons for him showing up late.

At times, she says that his friends make him late,

while other times, she says my grandma
makes him late.

Sometimes she says...
His car has broken down, that is why
he is late.

...And every year new excuses,

excuses,

excuses,

and
more
excuses...

I think, grandpa is hiding something
from me.

Oh! what could he be
hiding from me?

Is he a detective?

'oh no, He is too noisy, clumsy and
would not be able to keep quiet or
stay still.

...Or Is he a monster hunter?
'oh no, it can not be! he will be too
scared of them and they will
frighten him.

...Or maybe a security guard
for Aliens?

'oh no, he would not understand
them and would get confused
on what they are uttering
to him.

Heb

Pex

oh! what could he beeeee!

I think, I have got it.

I- know exactly what he is.
He is the,

Eidi man!!!!!

wooohoo! what a magnificent
and also prefect job for grandpa.

As he takes pleasure on giving presents.
Especially, to less fortunate
and not so wealthy.

To spread joy, happiness and sparkle
a smile on people's faces on a
festive day.

Now! that is my grandpa, whom
I know.

Eidi man, must have the coolest rides
for every season of Eid so he can
carry all the lovely gifts.

For a summer Eid.
I am guessing he would
ride an air balloon.

So, it will keep him breezy and cool.

On a spring Eid.

It would be a Minibus.

So, he could see all the beautiful sights
as he drives around to do deliveries.

On an Autumn Eid.

He would ride on a spaceship with
the strongest legs, which will grip
on the ground firmly.
So, that the mighty wind does not
blow the splendid spaceship
away.

...And for a winter Eid.
I can imagine, a horse carriage.
So, it would not skid on icy roads and
he would not have a terrible fall.

I believe the people he visits or creatures he meets, must be waiting for this day with a full on merrily spirits.

As with children at the shelters or other places. They get overly excited as they welcome him.

As for homeless, they get hopeful and can not wait to unwrap their goodies.

...And the animals on street hovering around him as they search for their special treats.

For now, I know.

My grandpa the Eidi man is busy
doing charity to bring smiles to
others also making the world
a happier place.
I don't mind him coming
home to me, a little
late.

Have a peaceful and joyous Eid, everyone.

Zara